No one shall make any changes in this title(s) for the purpose of production. No part of this book may be reproduced, stored in a retrieval system, scanned, uploaded, or transmitted in any form, by any means, now known or yet to be invented, including mechanical, electronic, digital, photocopying, recording, videotaping, or otherwise, without the prior written permission of the publisher. No one shall share this title(s), or any part of this title(s), through any social media or file hosting websites.

For all inquiries regarding motion picture, television, online/digital and other media rights, please contact Concord Theatricals Corp.

MUSIC AND THIRD-PARTY MATERIALS USE NOTE

Licensees are solely responsible for obtaining formal written permission from copyright owners to use copyrighted music and/or other copyrighted third-party materials (e.g. artworks, logos) in the performance of this play and are strongly cautioned to do so. If no such permission is obtained by the licensee, then the licensee must use only original music and materials that the licensee owns and controls. Licensees are solely responsible and liable for clearances of all third-party copyrighted materials, including without limitation music, and shall indemnify the copyright owners of the play(s) and their licensing agent, Concord Theatricals Corp., against any costs, expenses, losses and liabilities arising from the use of such copyrighted third-party materials by licensees. For music, please contact the appropriate music licensing authority in your territory for the rights to any incidental music.

IMPORTANT BILLING AND CREDIT REQUIREMENTS

If you have obtained performance rights to this title, please refer to your licensing agreement for important billing and credit requirements.

Rehearsal Tracks and Lead Sheets are available upon request from Concord Theatricals for the following songs: *Distractiuons, Hyper-Focus, Like Song,* and *More Than This.*

HYPER-FOCUS was first produced by the Playwrights Project in schools and community centers throughout San Diego, Orange and Los Angeles counties on October 24, 2004. The performance was directed by Robert May and D. Candis Paule, with sets by Beeb Salzer, costumes by Martha Phillips, sound by Rachel Le Vine, techincal direction by Luke Skoug, and scenic painting by Torrey Hyman. The Production Stage Manager was Diep Huynh. The cast was as follows:

T.J. . . . . .Tommy Friedman

MOM, ENSEMBLE . . . . Barbara Cole

COUNSELOR, SANDY, ENSEMBLE . . . . Jeannine Marquie

DR. SIGMUND, MR. FRANKLIN,

     DAD, TEACHER, ENSEMBLE. . . . . John Nutten

TEACHER, ENSEMBLE . . . . Wanetah Walmsley

Playwrights Project produced *Hyper-Focus* as its WINS Tour (Writers In the Next Stage of their careers) performed at schools and community centers throughout San Diego, Orange County and Los Angeles in Fall 2004.

Playwrights Project is a San Diego based non-profit arts education organization, founded by Deborah Salzer in 1985. Its mission is to advance literacy, creativity, and communication by empowering individuals to voice their stories through playwriting programs and theatre productions. Programs include in-school playwriting workshops for grades four-twelve; an annual statewide playwriting competition for writers under age nineteen; professional productions of Plays by Young Writers; touring productions; teacher training; dramaturgical work with young adult playwrights; and programs for special populations, including foster youth and seniors.

CHARACTERS

ACTOR 1 – T.J. – His mother named him Thomas Jefferson. Play ages nine-fourteen.

ACTOR 2 – MOM (T.J.'s Mom) – Literature Teacher.

ACTOR 3 – Teacher, Girl, Math Teacher.

ACTOR 4 – Principal, Sigmund, Science Teacher, Mr. Franklin, Dad.

ACTOR 5 – Counselor, Sandy.

The Distractions, The Seratones and The Declarations.

AUTHOR'S NOTES

I first wrote *Hyper-Focus* in 2004 as my second of three commissioned young audience plays for the Playwrights Project in California. The main topic of the play was assigned to me: ADHD. Everything else was for me to figure out. While I myself have never been diagnosed with ADHD, I had close friends who were and so I started my research by talking with them about their experiences in school, with their diagnosis, and through being medicated. I was fortunate enough to be able to work with neuroscientists and ADHD experts as well, to make sure I got the medical details correct.

Ultimately, the play was produced and toured through Southern California schools, libraries, and other public centers, first in 2004 and then again in 2008. The actors were all adults, some of them playing kids. The audiences were mainly middle school and high school students. Picture five actors in a van with a stage manager and a folding set that went to different locations and would sometimes put on one–three assembly-length shows in a row, then pack it all up and do it again the next day. Picture the audience often sitting on the floor of their gymnasium watching the show and participating in a talk back about ADHD afterwards.

Since then, the play has been produced around the country at various schools. I heard about productions but was never close enough to go see them. I'm sure they were amazing and my thanks goes to everyone who has produced this play!

In the summer of 2022, a theater director named Kyle Reynolds, from a school closer to where I live called Kingswood Oxford School, contacted me about producing the play. I had been feeling that it could use some revision after nearly two decades, especially in regards to the way we talk about ADHD and also in the way we talk about Thomas Jefferson – acknowledging that while he wrote the Declaration of Independence and is central among the major figures in the founding era, he also was a plantation owner who held people as slaves. That's a lot to tackle in a thirty-minute play, but I felt it was necessary and quickly realized that

this school production could help me greatly in updating this play for the roaring 2020s.

I am grateful to so many people at KO. Kyle helped me connect first with the very smart and talented high school cast, then the wellness team of the school to get their feedback on the contemporary understanding of ADHD (which is never called ADD now, as opposed to in 2004), and then the history department to discuss how and where to address the subject of the historical Thomas Jefferson in the context of this play.

I got to see two performances of the play in November 2022, each followed by an audience talkback, for which I sat on a panel with a neuroscientist, school counselors, two very brave students with ADHD, and one of their mothers. There was even an adult audience member who brought up a point about dopamine that spurred further refinement of the script with the help of my new neuroscientist friend. This production underlined for me what this play always was and always should be: a communal experience in empathy and education.

This is a play about what it is like to grow up with ADHD and the process of figuring out how to deal with it, and it is especially about surrounding yourself with people who care about you and are trying to help, whether or not they are experts in what you are going through.

That said, if you are producing the play, have fun with it! It's meant to be fast and rambunctious, punctuated by moments of sincere connection.

Kids playing adults: feel free to satirize the ones that seem ridiculous and also to delve deeply into the ones who seem like they are really trying to make a difference.

Adults, if you're playing kids: remember what it was like growing up. It's hard even without having to deal with ADHD!

Directors: This is meant to be a very physical play with a lot of movement, but sometimes it comes into crystal clear focus, all title reference intended.

Designers: You get to visualize what it's like to have a brain that is always finding something new to be fascinated by.

Musicians and music directors: Music is essential to this play. You can present it as makes the most sense to you, but the songs are written, ahem, by me, so stick to the music provided, whether it be with your own instrumentalists or any backing tracks.

Thank you for being part of this play with all of us!

Jim Knable
Brooklyn, 2023

(**T.J.** *is on stage with his guitar, like he's working
out a song.*)

T.J.

AND I'M HYPER
AND I'M FOCUSED
AND I'M...HYPER-FOCUSED
THEN I COME BACK DOWN
AND THERE'S LOVE ALL AROUND
AND I REALIZE THERE'S NOTHING THAT'S HOPELESS...

(*He looks up and takes in the audience, putting
his guitar away and getting into the scene.*)

I've always had a hard time concentrating. Especially
in class. Ever since I started school, I would sit at my
desk, the teacher would start talking...

(*Enter* **TEACHER.**)

TEACHER. Good morning, boys and girls, I'm your teacher
Mrs. Schmickelpennick.

T.J. And she would keep talking, but what I was hearing
and seeing in my head was...

(*The* **DISTRACTIONS** *enter, actors who act out
various objects and beings in the following song.
The song starts moderately, but gets crazier and
crazier in tempo and intensity as the millions of
distractions in T.J.'s world vie for his attention.*)

PAY ATTENTION TO ME,
I'M THE CLOCK ON THE WALL,
JUST A-SPINNIN' MY HANDS
IN A CIRCULAR BALL
PAY ATTENTION TO ME,
I'M A BIRD IN A TREE
JUST A-CHIRPIN' A TWEET
'CAUSE IT MAKES ME FEEL FREE

DISTRACTIONS. *(Cont.)*
> I'M THE PENCIL AND THE STENCIL AND THE CLOUD
>> THAT'S OUT THE WINDOW
> I'M THE LACE THAT'S ON YOUR SHOE THAT'S LEFT UNTIED
> I'M THE TEACHER, I'M YOUR T-SHIRT, I'M THE WRINKLES,
>> I'M THE CREASES
> PAY ATTENTION OVER HERE I'LL CATCH YOUR EYE!

TEACHER. Thomas? Thomas Jeffereson.

(The song continues.)

DISTRACTIONS.
> I'M THE FLUORESCENT LIGHTS
> BLINKIN' FLICKERIN FAST
> BUZZIN' OUT LIKE HUM
> WHILE YOU SIT AT YOUR DESK
> I'M THE CREAK OF YOUR CHAIR,
> I'M THE SPRINKLERS OUTSIDE
> I'M A FLY IN YOUR EAR
> I'M THE GUY ON YOUR RIGHT
>
> I'M THE END OF YOUR ERASER, I'M THE STAPLES IN THE
>> STAPLER
> I'M THE CRACK THAT RUNS ALONG THE CLASSROOM
>> FLOOR
> I'M THE FISH IN THE AQUARIUM THE SPLISH IN YOUR
>> SPLASHARIUM
> LOOK OVER HERE, LOOK OVER HERE, LOOK OVER HERE
>> SOME MORE!

TEACHER. Thomas Jefferson!

*(The **DISTRACTIONS** scatter.)*

T.J. Here. *(to us)* Yes, my name is Thomas Jefferson. My last name's Jefferson and my mom named me Thomas because she said she had great expectations for me. I like to be called T.J.

TEACHER. Would you lead the class in the pledge of allegiance, Thomas?

T.J. Uh, okay. *(He stands at his desk.)* I pledge allegiance to the flag of the United States of America, one nation, invisible –

TEACHER. Indivisible.

T.J. Indivisible, and the Republic for which it stands. *(He stops.)* One nation, indivisible. Invisible. Invincible. What does that word mean?

TEACHER. What word?

T.J. Invincible. How do I know that word?

TEACHER. You're going backwards, Thomas. The republic for which it stands...

T.J. *(Figuring it out.)* It's invisible like the Invisible Man...

TEACHER. Indivisible! Come on, now, Thomas, you can finish it.

T.J. Invincible means strong, doesn't it?

TEACHER. Yes, but you already passed that part.

T.J. What part?

TEACHER. Indivisible! One Union...

T.J. Does indivisible mean one union?

TEACHER. It doesn't matter, just say it!

T.J. Why should I say it if I don't know what it means?

TEACHER. Do you want to go to the principal, Thomas?

T.J. What did I do? I didn't do anything.

TEACHER. Go to the principal, young man.

T.J. Why? That's not fair! What did I do?!

TEACHER. You know exactly what you did. Go!

    (**TEACHER** *exits.*)

T.J. I was always getting sent to the principal.

    (**PRINCIPAL** *enters, a very silly-looking man.*)

PRINCIPAL. Well, hello, Mr. Jefferson. First day of school, huh? *(Looks at his watch.)* First five minutes. I think that's a record.

T.J. I didn't do anything.

PRINCIPAL. Your teacher says you were disrupting the class.

T.J. That's not true.

PRINCIPAL. Are you calling Mrs. Schmickelpennick a liar?

T.J. No, I never said...

PRINCIPAL. I'm calling your mother.

T.J. *(To us.)* No, please...

> (**PRINCIPAL** *pulls out a phone.* **MOM** *enters, on her phone.)*

MOM. My son would never disrupt class on purpose. He's a good boy.

PRINCIPAL. He causes trouble. He did it all last year and now he's doing it before the first day's even half over.

MOM. He doesn't mean to cause trouble. He's just very smart and talks before he thinks...

PRINCIPAL. He's a discipline problem, ma'am.

T.J. Which is what he said all last year. I was a bad kid, that's what they all said.

PRINCIPAL. Your son is out of control. I'm recommending he see the school counselor.

T.J. And then Mom started crying. I could hear her over the phone. I was always making her cry. No matter what I did, I couldn't stop it from happening. I was bad. Even though I was always trying not to be. I was like a werewolf. Like in the old movie.

> (**MOM** *and* **PRINCIPAL** *exit.)*

Like the man who turns into a werewolf who doesn't want to turn into a werewolf, but then the moon comes out –

(A moon appears. **T.J.** *gets more and more worked up, turning into a werewolf.)*

And he feels the little prickles under his skin. His teeth turn into fangs, his whole body turns hairy, he grows claws on his fingers, he runs outside into the woods and –

> (**MOM** *enters.)*

MOM. Thomas.

> (**T.J.** *freezes in mid-attack pose.)*

T.J. Yes.

MOM. What are you doing?

T.J. Turning into a werewolf.

MOM. Do you want to talk about what happened in class today?

(**T.J.** *straightens up and faces his mother.*)

T.J. She isn't fair. I hate her.

MOM. Who?

T.J. The teacher. I was just asking questions.

MOM. And then...

T.J. And then she got frustrated and the class started laughing and she couldn't make them stop, so she sent me to the principal.

MOM. You might have been talking to her in a way that hurt her feelings.

T.J. I wasn't.

MOM. Listen to me, Thomas. The principal thinks it's a good idea if you talk to a very nice woman at your school who likes to help kids solve their problems.

T.J. I don't have any problems.

(**MOM** *looks like she might cry again.*)

Okay, Mom, I'll talk to her. I'll talk to anyone. It's okay.

MOM. I love you more than anything, Thomas.

(*She goes to him and hugs him.*)

T.J. I love you, too, Mom. Can I watch TV now?

MOM. Did you do your homework?

T.J. I did it at the After-School Program. When you were late picking me up.

MOM. Okay, you can watch TV But nothing violent.

(**MOM** *kisses* **T.J.***'s head and then exits.*)

T.J. Later that week, I met with the school counselor.

(**COUNSELOR** *enters, a friendly woman with big glasses.*)

COUNSELOR. Hello, Thomas.

T.J. Hello.

COUNSELOR. Do you like to be called Thomas?

T.J. I like to be called T.J.

COUNSELOR. T.J. How are you feeling today?

T.J. Fine.

COUNSELOR. Do you know why you're talking to me?

T.J. I'm a discipline problem.

COUNSELOR. *(laughs)* Who said that?

T.J. Everyone. I don't try to cause trouble, it just happens and I get blamed for it. It's not fair.

COUNSELOR. Do you have a hard time paying attention to things in class?

T.J. Sometimes I get bored.

COUNSELOR. And your mind wanders. You think about a lot of other things. Sometimes you just have to get up and start walking around in the middle of class.

T.J. Sometimes.

COUNSELOR. And then you get in trouble?

T.J. Yeah, but it's not my fault.

COUNSELOR. I understand.

(*Pause.*)

T.J. You do?

COUNSELOR. I'm going to talk to your teacher and try to explain things to her.

T.J. You're going to talk to her?

COUNSELOR. Yes. And then you and I will meet again in a little while. How does that sound?

T.J. Good.

(*Turns to us,* **COUNSELOR** *exits.*)

She wasn't even mad at me. She seemed to understand. And Mrs. Schmickelpennick was nicer to me. Until one day when everything went wrong:

(**T.J.** *takes his seat at a desk.* **TEACHER** *enters.* **T.J.** *fidgets while she talks.*)

TEACHER. Now class, I don't want you to be nervous. But it's time to take the test on your multiplication tables. I'm going to call you up one by one and you'll stand up at your desk and say them. Thomas?

T.J. Huh?

TEACHER. Are you ready?

T.J. For what?

TEACHER. To say your multiplication tables.

T.J. Why?

TEACHER. Didn't you hear what I just said?

T.J. When?

TEACHER. Just now. It's time to take the test. Stand up, please.

T.J. *(Very nervous.)* Test?

TEACHER. All you have do is say one times one is one, one times two is two, one times three...

*(The **DISTRACTIONS** enter again holding various numbers that they spin and hurl around.)*

DISTRACTION 1. One times one is one times one is one times one is one times one.

DISTRACTION 2. *(Over **DISTRACTION 1**)* Times two is two times two is four times four is forty-two times two is twoty-forty, seventy seven, eleven is...

DISTRACTION 1. Tooty-fruity on the rudy, I don't know what to dooty, Tooty-fruity!

DISTRACTION 2. A wop-bop-a-lu-bob-a-wop-bam boo!

TEACHER. Thomas!

*(The **DISTRACTIONS** run off. **T.J.** looks a deer caught in the headlights.)*

Why don't you just try it?

T.J. No.

TEACHER. No?

T.J. I don't want to.

(He sits down.)

TEACHER. Do you want to go to the principal, young man?

T.J. No, but...

TEACHER. You have an attitude problem. Stand and say your tables or go to the principal.

(**T.J.** *stands defiantly, angry.*)

T.J. One times one is one. One times two is a big brown shoe. One times three is little green pea. One times four is you're a big bore and I don't have to listen to you anymore!

(**TEACHER** *reacts with a silent and frozen pose of an angry god hurling down cruel retribution. To us:*)

To make a long story short, the next thing I knew my mom and I were meeting with the counselor.

(**TEACHER** *exits.* **MOM** *and* **COUNSELOR** *enter.*)

COUNSELOR. It's very good to meet you, Mrs. Jefferson.

MOM. Nice to meet you. My son is not a bad boy.

COUNSELOR. I know. He's a very good well-intentioned bright young man. He just has a hard time focusing and sitting still in class. Right, T.J.?

T.J. I guess.

COUNSELOR. I would like to suggest that he be evaluated for ADHD.

T.J. (*To us.*) I didn't know what that meant, but it sounded like a disease and I got really scared. I had some kind of disease that was rotting my brain and making me crazy. I pictured brown slime oozing out of my ears and strange warts all over my body and...

COUNSELOR. T.J. I don't want you to feel like I'm saying you have some strange disease. ADHD stands for Attention Deficit Hyper-Activity disorder. It's a condition that many kids and adults have. It makes it hard to stay focused. It makes you fidgety in class. I'm not qualified to diagnose it, but I know someone who can. A friend of mine. A psychiatrist.

T.J. *(To us, freaking out.)* A psychiatrist?!

(**SIGMUND**, *a psychiatrist, enters.* **COUNSELOR** *exits.)*

SIGMUND. Hello Thomas, Hello Mrs. Jefferson. I am Doctor Sigmund.

MOM. I let him watch TV I let him watch TV after he finishes his homework. Is that why he might have ADD?

SIGMUND. First of all, we call it ADHD now. Second, no one knows exactly how anyone gets it. The only thing we do know is that it's often passed down through families. Have you or your husband ever been diagnosed?

MOM. I don't actually have a husband.

SIGMUND. T.J.'s father.

MOM. Thomas's father was a train engineer. He's not alive anymore. I'm sure he didn't have ADD. He couldn't. He definitely had to concentrate to drive a train.

SIGMUND. *(correcting her)* ADHD. He probably learned to hyper-focus.

MOM & T.J. Hyper-Focus?

SIGMUND. It's one of many tools that people dealing with ADHD have. You can block out all distractions and focus on one thing at a time. But we can talk about that later. I would like to give Thomas a few little tests that will help us figure out if it is ADHD to begin with.

T.J. Tests? I don't want to take any tests.

SIGMUND. Okay, no tests. I'll just ask you a few questions and show you some pictures and talk. I'm not grading you, I'm just curious. Okay?

T.J. Yeah.

SIGMUND. Do you always feel like you need to move some part of your body when you're sitting down? Like what you're doing right now with your leg?

T.J. What? That? Oh, I don't know. Maybe.

SIGMUND. I do it, too. Look at what I'm doing with my pen. See how I keep bouncing it off the table? I understand

that you have a hard time with your handwriting...

(Scene freezes.)

T.J. *(To us.)* He asked me a lot of questions like that and had me read some things and tell him what I read. And then we looked at pictures. When he was done he said:

(Scene unfreezes.)

SIGMUND. I do think that T.J. has ADHD and I think he would benefit from medication.

MOM. *(To him.)* Medication?

T.J. *(To us.)* Medication?

SIGMUND. Let me explain it to you. *(He pulls out a large cardboard brain poster.)* Dopamine, norepinephrine, serotonin: they're all neurotransmitters. Neurotransmitters are what help your brain communicate with itself. Kids and adults who have ADHD have neurotransmitters that aren't doing their jobs. What medications do is help your neurotransmiters work better by raising their levels for a certain amount of time. If you figure out the right combination of medication for your individual brain, then you'll find it's easier to concentrate, to focus, even just to stay still when you need to.

T.J. Dopa what? Who?

SIGMUND. Dopamine.

And I have some ideas for other things that might help along with the meds...

T.J. *(Tuning out* **SIGMUND,** *to us.)* I was sick, something was wrong with my brain, just like I was afraid of. What would all the kids at school say if they found out?

*(***GIRL [TEACHER]** *pops out.)*

GIRL. Med-head! Brain-drain! Freako-Sicko-Creepo-Disease Boy!

(She disappears.)

T.J. No one must ever know. I have to keep this secret. I have to –

SIGMUND. Thomas?

T.J. Huh?

SIGMUND. You just had a space-out, didn't you?

T.J. A what.

SIGMUND. Some people call it a blink. It's like you just left the room and went somewhere else and now you're back and you have to figure out what happened while you were gone. That happens to you a lot, doesn't it?

T.J. I don't know, I guess. Can we go home now?

(To us.)

I didn't want to talk about it anymore. I just wanted to be alone in my room.

*(**SIGMUND** and **MOM** leave.)*

I want to hide. I don't want to see anyone. I want to live in a cave. I want to dress up like a cave man and make cave paintings and eat animals and talk in grunts. If I talked like ugh, ugh nobody would know when I had a space out or a blink or left the room. And no one would care about my handwriting. And I wouldn't have ADDHD or whatever you call it! Ugh! Ugh! Ugh!

*(**MOM** enters.)*

MOM. Thomas?

T.J. Ugh?

MOM. Are you okay?

T.J. Yeah.

MOM. Are you being a werewolf?

T.J. Cave man.

MOM. Pretty big day, huh? You probably have a lot you're thinking about.

Look, I have something I want to give you. I was going to wait until you were older, but I think you might be ready for it now and Dr. Sigmund thinks it might be good for you. *(She produces a guitar.)* It belonged to your father.

(**T.J.** *takes it carefully.*)

T.J. He played music?

MOM. He was very good.

T.J. Did he leave this guitar for me to have?

MOM. Yes. Do you want to learn to play it?

(**T.J.** *nods.*)

It'll take some hard work to learn. You'll have to concentrate. Focus.

T.J. Okay, I'll do it.

MOM. I know you will. We'll get through this together.

T.J. Get through what?

(**MOM** *kisses him on the head and exits. All of* **T.J.***'s attention in focused on the guitar now.*)

I could barely remember what I had been so upset about. All I could think about was the guitar. It felt so cool in my hands. My guitar. My father gave it to me. He died before I was born, but he knew I would need this. That I was destined to be...A ROCK STAR!

(**PRINCIPAL** *sets up standing mic, first talking into it, then letting* **T.J.** *take it over.*)

PRINCIPAL. And now, ladies and gentlemen, T.J. and the Dopatones!

(**T.J.** *starts strumming on his guitar and steps to the mic.*)

(*The* **DOPATONES** *enter* (**COUNSELOR** *and* **GIRL,** *in sunglasses and cool jackets*).

[SONG: MORE THAN THIS]

I'M SO FRUSTRATED
I JUST CAN'T TAKE IT
NOTHIN' I EVER DO
EVER MAKES SENSE

I GOT SO MUCH IN ME
I GOT SO MUCH ENERGY

BUT WHEN IT COMES, IT COMES OUT LIKE THIS

MY MIND IS SO BIG THAT I CAN'T SEE IT ALL
MY EYES ARE SO BIG, I SEE THROUGH IT

I'M NOT STUPID
I JUST CAN'T DO IT
I WANT TO BE MORE THAN THIS

I TRY SO HARD, BUT NO ONE EVEN KNOWS
JUST HOW HARD IT IS

I'M NOT STUPID
I JUST CAN'T DO IT
I WANT TO BE MORE THAN THIS

(He finishes. Applause, applause. **PRINCIPAL** *enters and speaks into the mic.)*

PRINCIPAL. Thank you, Thomas, that was a…unique contribution to this year's talent show. Judges?

*(***TEACHER*** *enters holding a large card on which "10" is written.)*

All 10's. Looks like you won first place. Congratulations, Thomas.

T.J. Pause.

*(***PRINCIPAL*** *and* ***TEACHER*** *freeze. To us:)*

I bet you think this is one of my fantasies. Nope. This actually happened. I just skipped ahead a couple years. This is from when I was in sixth grade. I learned how to play guitar and started writing my own songs. A lot of things happened by then. You're just going to have to catch up and figure out what. Which is what I have to do all the time.

*(***PRINCIPAL*** *and* ***TEACHER*** *unfreeze.)*

PRINCIPAL. And while I don't condone rock and roll, I do think it's impressive that you wrote your own song, Thomas. I remember when you used to come into my office when you were in third grade…

T.J. I wasn't paying attention to what he was saying by that

point because I got distracted. Out in the audience there was this girl in the other sixth grade class for gifted and talented students looking up at me like I'd never seen a girl looking up at me.

*(A girl, **SANDY**, enters and demonstrates. She obviously has her first serious crush on a musician.)*

T.J. *(Cont.)* It made me feel really weird and I felt my face getting hot and my stomach sort of shaking. She just kept looking at me. I didn't even know her.

PRINCIPAL. Thomas?

*(**THOMAS** snaps out of it and looks at **PRINCIPAL**.)*

Keep up the good work.

*(**PRINCIPAL** pats him on the back and exits with **TEACHER**.*

*(**THOMAS** is left alone with **SANDY**.)*

SANDY. Hi.

T.J. Hi.

SANDY. That was really good. Your song. Do you really feel like that?

T.J. No, it's just a song.

SANDY. My name's Sandy.

T.J. I'm T.J.

SANDY. *(giggles)* I know. I couldn't believe all those things Principal Hanaman was saying about you. And when he said he'd really miss you next year...

T.J. He said that?

SANDY. Yeah, didn't you hear him?

T.J. Sure.

SANDY. So what middle school are you going to?

T.J. George Washington.

SANDY. *(obviously thrilled)* Really? I mean, me too. I guess we'll keep seeing each other. I mean, you know, maybe

we'll have a class together. Are you going to take band or something? Because I might.

T.J. I haven't thought about it.

SANDY. Oh, okay. Well. I really liked your song. Hey, what does T.J. stand for?

T.J. Thomas Jefferson.

SANDY. Like the one on the nickel?

T.J. Yeah.

SANDY. Cool. I guess I'll see you around, Thomas.

(She quickly and awkwardly kisses him on the cheek then runs away.)

T.J. And that was the first time I actually liked it when somebody called me Thomas.

*(****MOM**** enters.)*

MOM. Thomas?

T.J. *(not thrilled to see her)* Hi, Mom.

MOM. That was so wonderful, honey. I'm so proud of you. First prize, look at you. I'm so proud.
Look, I think you might have forgotten to take your meds this morning, I brought them for you.

T.J. No, Mom, not here!

MOM. Did you forget?

T.J. Put them away! Don't let anyone see you give me those.

MOM. Can you just tell me if you took one or not?

T.J. No. I didn't. And I don't need to. Bye.

*(****T.J.**** exits. ****MOM**** exits after him. ****T.J.**** reenters.)*

All right, so not everything was great. I was taking a kind of medication that you take to help you calm down and concentrate. I guess it made me calmer, but it did other weird things to me. Like it made me not hungry all day and then starving all night. I guess it helped me, but I didn't want anyone to know about it. It was bad enough that whenever we had to take a test or quiz, I had to go to a separate room and have twice

as much time as everyone else to finish. But I would be so embarrassed if anyone knew I had to take pills to make myself normal. And there she was, my Mom, just handing them to me right where everyone could see.

*(***MOM*** enters.)*

MOM. It's normal, the feelings you're having. Most boys have a father around when they're growing up. You just have me and sometimes you get frustrated.

T.J. No, that's not it.

MOM. What is it then?

T.J. I don't want to take the pills anymore.

MOM. Thomas, come here. Sit down.
It was very hard for me to decide that you needed the medication. I was afraid I would be doing the wrong thing. But the doctor said it would help you, so I decided we should try it, and, Thomas, it has helped you. I can tell that it's easier for you to focus now. Your grades are much better. You don't get in trouble as much. And, honey, look what you can do with your guitar...

T.J. Are you saying I couldn't play guitar if I didn't take pills?

MOM. No, no, not at all. I'm just saying I can tell that it's easier for you. When you're a parent you want things to be as good and easy for your kids as they can be. That's all I want. If you really want to try not taking the medication, we can try to do that, too. I just want you to be able to do everything you want and nothing to get in your way. I love you more than anything, Thomas.
It hurts me when you talk to me like you did today at your school.

T.J. I'm sorry.

MOM. Okay. Thank you.
So who was that girl you were talking to?

T.J. (*Blushing and shutting down.*) Nobody.

(*He walks off.*)

MOM. Thomas…

(*She sighs and goes after him.*)

(**SANDY** *enters from opposite.*)

SANDY. Thomas!

(**T.J.** *enters with a backpack.*)

T.J. Hey.

(*Turns to us.*)

Four months later. The first day of middle school.

SANDY. Are you ready?

T.J. Ready?

SANDY. For the first day. Different teachers for different classes. Gym.

T.J. I guess.

SANDY. How was your summer?

T.J. Uh. Good.

SANDY. That's so cool.

(*Awkward pause.*)

I mean… Did you write any new songs?

T.J. Um, Yeah.

SANDY. I'd really like to hear one. Sometime. If you ever wanted to play one. For me.
Okay, well, bye.

(*She ducks out shyly.*)

T.J. This time I felt like there was glue in my mouth that made it so I couldn't say anything. My face was all hot. My eyes were kind of bulging out of my head like two tennis balls. At least that's what it felt like.
I *had* written a new song that summer. Ever since I wrote it, all I did was imagine singing it to her.

(*His guitar and microphone are set up for him quickly.*)

[SONG: LIKE SONG]

T.J. *(Cont.)*
> I DON'T KNOW YOU
> BUT I ALWAYS WANTED TO
> HOW YOU LOOK AT ME
> IS HOW I ALWAYS WANT TO BE
> EVERY NIGHT I DREAM
> THAT YOU MIGHT LIKE ME
> WHAT SHOULD I DO
> I THINK I LIKE YOU

(Strike the guitar and mic.)

But how the heck could I ever sing that to her?

It was going to be a very big year. A whole new school. Lots of different people.

Lots of different kinds of classes to keep track of. I was scared to death.

(**MATH TEACHER [COUNSELOR]** *enters.*)

MATH TEACHER. Good morning, class. We're going to start by doing long division backwards and squared times the triple quadratic equation root of the Roman numeral I.

(**SCIENCE TEACHER [PRINCIPAL]** *enters with two glass beakers full of orange liquid, talking in a high funny voice.*)

SCIENCE TEACHER. Hello pupils, today we're going to mix these two chemicals together to make a frog, which we will then dissect with a very sharp table of elements.

(**LITERATURE TEACHER [MOM]** *enters.*)

LITERATURE TEACHER. I would like you all to read the complete works of William Shakespeare by tomorrow and be ready to name all the characters in reverse alphabetical order.

MATH TEACHER. Combining numerators and denominators into trigonometric obtuse right angles…

SCIENCE TEACHER. And then we're going to map the universe with rabbits and learn what they eat...

LITERATURE TEACHER. While diagramming compound sentences into advanced vocabulary pronouns...

MATH TEACHER. Which will all be on the test on Monday...

SCIENCE TEACHER. And you'll be tested once a week...

LITERATURE TEACHER. And graded on your use of multi-syllabic words and handwriting.

MATH TEACHER. But for tonight's homework...

SCIENCE TEACHER. I want you to construct a balsa wood structure strong enough to hold...

LITERATURE. The Encyclopedia Brittanica,

ALL TEACHERS. Is that clear?

*(***T.J.*** screams, covers his ears and closes his eyes.)*

*(The ***TEACHERS*** all run off.)*

T.J. I decided to run away that night. I would run away to the woods and live out in a little house and cook hot dogs and...

*(***MOM*** enters.)*

MOM. So, how was the first day?

T.J. Okay.

MOM. Pretty scary, huh?

T.J. No. A little.

MOM. I remember my first day of middle school. I couldn't find my English classroom and had to ask everyone where it was, only it turned out I had read my schedule backwards and had already missed it.

T.J. That's nice, Mom.

MOM. I know. It's harder for you. Did you see your old friends from last year?

T.J. I don't have any friends from last year.

MOM. How about teachers? Did you like any of them?

T.J. No.
Well...
There was one.

(**MR. FRANKLIN [PRINCIPAL]** *enters. He looks suspiciously like old B.F. himself, even has a Revolutionary era wig.*)

(*He reads from a roll book.*)

MR. FRANKLIN. Thomas Jefferson. Thomas. Jefferson.

(**T.J.** *moves into* **FRANKLIN***'s scene.*)

T.J. Here. I like to be called T.J.

MR. FRANKLIN. Uh-huh. I knew another Thomas Jefferson once. Heck of a guy. We hung out in France together. I gave him a little advice on an essay he was writing. It was more like a declaration really. How did it go?
We hold these truths to be self-evident, that all men are created equal, that they are endowed by their Creator with certain unalienable Rights, that among these are Life, Liberty and the pursuit of Happiness.
Heck of a guy. I wouldn't mind being called Thomas Jefferson if I were you. I know it's a lot of weight on your shoulders. But I suspect that you could take it.

(*He exits.*)

T.J. Mr. Franklin. I kinda liked him. He was different. Funny. But he seemed like he really cared about the stuff he was teaching. It was easier to pay attention to him.
I liked the way the Declaration of Independence sounded when he started saying it.

MOM. Thomas Jefferson wrote that.

T.J. *I know*, Mom.

MOM. And they all know about your needs, your teachers. You gave them the notes?

T.J. (*Brought down.*) Yeah. Yeah, Mom. They know about my *special needs*.

(**T.J.** *starts to walk off.*)

MOM. Thomas!

(*He looks back in anger.*)

I don't like it when you walk away from me like that.

T.J. I don't like how everything is always about my little problem.

MOM. I'm sorry if it seems like that, I thought you were talking about –

T.J. I wasn't. I was just talking about my day like a normal person.

MOM. Okay. Forgive me. Maybe sometime you'll ask me about my day before you just eat your dinner and go off to your room.

(Pause.)

T.J. What?

MOM. Nothing. Sorry. I'm making macaroni. Is that okay?

T.J. Mom?

MOM. Yes?

T.J. Are you okay?

MOM. I had a hard day, too.

T.J. What happened?

MOM. I don't want to...

I got laid off from my job.

*(**T.J.** just looks at her, not knowing what he's supposed to say.)*

It's okay. It'll be okay. I have a bunch of ideas. I've gone through this before. You don't have to worry about anything. I just had a hard day, too, and then you walked away from me like that and...

*(**T.J.** goes up to his **MOM** and hugs her.)*

Thank you, sweetie.

T.J. I have some money from the lawns I mowed this summer.

MOM. Oh, Thomas. You're the greatest, sweetest, most beautiful boy... young man. I have a great feeling about this year for you. I think you'll find all kinds of new things to enjoy and new ways to deal with the hard stuff.

T.J. And you will, too.

MOM. Yes. I will. Come on, kid, let's cook up some dinner.

(They go off.)

(SANDY *enters, reading a paper.)*

SANDY. The most embarrassing thing that ever happened to my friend Betsy was when she was talking to a boy she thought was very talented and she made a total fool out of herself.

(T.J. *appears.)*

T.J. Sandy and I were both in creative writing class.

SANDY. She thinks he thinks she's stupid. She wishes she could tell him how she feels about him.

T.J. For some reason, I had the feeling that she was talking about herself and me.

SANDY. Maybe someday, she'll be brave enough. The end.

(SANDY *looks awkwardly at* **T.J.** *and then exits.)*

T.J. I was thinking about her all the time. Not even the medication could stop me from getting distracted in class thinking about her. I didn't know what I was supposed to do, though. Every time we talked, I felt weird afterwards, like I was doing it wrong. I wished my Dad was there to give me advice. I used to imagine what he'd say.

(DAD [PRINCIPAL] *enters, dressed like a train engineer, cap pulled down over his eyes.)*

DAD. You got to talk to her like you're proud of yourself. But at the same time, not too proud. And you got to tell her she's pretty, only don't let her know how much you like her. And if she tries to kiss you, you should act like you expected it, even if it surprises you. And you should make sure to move your lips a little when you're kissing, like they do in the new movies, but hold her like they do in the old movies.

T.J. I imagined him all the time growing up. But it was just now that I started picturing what kind of things he might actually say to me.

DAD. Go get her, son.

(He exits.)

T.J. I always wished I knew him. Always.

*(**SANDY** enters.)*

SANDY. Hi.

T.J. Oh, hi. I – um, liked your story.

SANDY. That happened to a friend of mine.

T.J. Yeah.

SANDY. Do you like your classes?

T.J. They're okay.

SANDY. Do you have Mr. Franklin? I heard he was really funny.

T.J. Yeah, he's cool.

SANDY. He dresses up and stuff right? Like he dressed up like someone from the American Revolution on the first day?

T.J. Benjamin Franklin.

SANDY. Is that his first name?

T.J. I don't know, but that's who he dressed up as.

SANDY. Are you going to the dance?

T.J. Dance?

SANDY. After school on Friday. I'm gonna go.

T.J. Yeah, maybe.

SANDY. Okay, well, bye.

(She exits.)

T.J. And I went.

(Something fun and vaguely appropriate plays.)

*(A couple other **KIDS** [**PRINCIPAL** and **TEACHER**] run on and start dancing around.)*

T.J. It was in the school cafeteria. The lights were dark and there were all these kids I didn't really know dancing around. I wanted to leave right away, but as I was walking towards the exit door...

*(**SANDY** runs on.)*

SANDY. Thomas!

(He turns to her.)

I didn't think you were gonna come. I couldn't find you before. I mean, I didn't see you around. Are you leaving?

T.J. Um...

(A slow dance song comes on.)

*(The other **KIDS** start to awkwardly slow dance with each other.)*

SANDY. Do you want to... I mean...

T.J. What.

SANDY. Dance or something.

T.J. Uh... I guess.

(They go to each other. They cautiously get into slow dance position and start swaying to the music. And then:)

SANDY. My friend Heidi said you have ADHD or something. Like you have to go outside the class to take tests. She told her mom about it and her Mom said you probably had dyslexia or ADHD.

*(**T.J.** looks mortified.)*

(He turns from her and starts off. She grabs his wrist.)

I just wanted you to know that I don't care. I think you're really cool. I want to know everything about you.

T.J. Let go of me.

(She does.)

It's all a lie. I don't have anything.

SANDY. But if you ever wanted to talk about it…

T.J. I gotta go.

SANDY. Thomas.

T.J. Don't call me Thomas. My name is T.J.

(He exits. She looks sadly after him and exits.)

*(**MOM** enters.)*

MOM. Thomas, dinner! Thomas!

*(**T.J.** enters miserably.)*

T.J. I don't want any, I'm not hungry.

MOM. What happened at the dance?

T.J. Nothing.

MOM. You're upset.

T.J. Nothing happened.

MOM. Was it that girl?

T.J. No! There's no girl!

MOM. Thomas?

T.J. NOTHING HAPPENED!

*(**MOM** throws up her hands and exits.)*

I wanted to tell her, but I couldn't. All I could think about was how embarrassed I was. That she knew. That everybody knew and they were all talking about me.

*(**GIRL** runs on with a newspaper.)*

GIRL. EXTRA, EXTRA, read all about it! T.J.'s got a bad case of ADHD love! He ran crying out of the first dance of the year! He can't even dance right!

(She disappears.)

T.J. The next day at school I didn't look at anyone. I knew I would see it in their eyes. What they all thought about me.

*(**MR. FRANKLIN** enters.)*

MR. FRANKLIN. Good morning, class. Today we're going to talk about Thomas Jefferson. The older one. He was one of our funkiest forefathers. I've put a little portrait of him on each of your desks. Yes, that nickel. There he is. Now flip that guy over and look at the tail end, if you would.

Do any one of you young historians know the name of that house on the back of the nickel? Monticello. Jefferson's house. You know who designed that house? You guessed it, T.J., himself. The, eh-hem, older T.J.

But he wasn't the one who built it. And he didn't do the physical work to run his plantation. That's the hard part in talking about Thomas Jefferson. His contradictions. How can a man who declares independence keep people as his slaves?

T.J. I was sitting in my favorite teacher's class, but I wasn't listening. I couldn't. I hadn't seen Sandy yet that day, but I knew I would have to in creative writing class. I never wanted to see her again, I hated her. Maybe I can say I'm sick so I won't have to go to creative writing.

MR. FRANKLIN. Our Mr. Jefferson is probably thinking about the next song he's going to write. Or maybe he's got Spring Fever…

T.J. I do not have Spring Fever, you big fat jerk.

MR. FRANKLIN. What? Thomas?

T.J. And I'm not anything like Thomas Jefferson. And you look stupid dressed up like a revolutionary guy. Everyone thinks you're silly. This class is stupid.

MR. FRANKLIN. Stop right there, Thomas, before you embarrass yourself any more. Step outside with me. Excuse me, class.

(The class goes away. They're outside.)

T.J. What! I'm going the principal's office. I know where it is. You don't have to take me.

MR. FRANKLIN. I'm not sending you to the principal's office.

T.J. But you told me to step outside.

MR. FRANKLIN. Because I wanted to talk to you in private. What's going on, son?

T.J. Don't you know? You read the note from my mom at the start of the year. You know what's wrong with me. Everybody does.

MR. FRANKLIN. Did someone make fun of you for it?

T.J. No, not really. But they know. This girl...

MR. FRANKLIN. Which girl?

T.J. This girl Sandy.

MR. FRANKLIN. Is Sandy a friend of yours?

T.J. No. Kind of. I don't know.

MR. FRANKLIN. So you do have Spring Fever.

T.J. No.

MR. FRANKLIN. And she figured out you were a little different? Had something you were hiding?

T.J. You could say that.

MR. FRANKLIN. What did she say to you? Something mean?

T.J. No. She said she didn't care. She said she wanted to know everything about me.

MR. FRANKLIN. Really? She sounds pretty special.

T.J. Yeah, but... No.

MR. FRANKLIN. I can pretty much guarantee you that she hasn't gone around gossiping behind your back. It sounds like she really cares about you.

T.J. Maybe, but...

MR. FRANKLIN. Listen, Thomas... T.J., you're a smart young dude. You've got something that gets in your way sometimes, something you try to hide so other people won't judge you by it. We've all got something like that. You want to know something about me, something that you'd probably never guess? I have ADHD, too.

T.J. What?

MR. FRANKLIN. I know exactly what you're going through.

T.J. You... have ADHD?

MR. FRANKLIN. Yeah. Surprised?

T.J. But you're a teacher. You're always focused.

MR. FRANKLIN. I'm glad you think so. But I'll tell you secret – don't tell the other kids: sometimes I totally space out, just like you. It's like we're in a special club, you and I. We've always got to be on our toes, always got to get right back into it, always trying our hardest to be our most aware. But you know what's just as important? Finding people in your life who care about you more than this obstacle. This girl sounds like one of those people. Your mom's one of those people. These people and the love they give you will help you get through anything. Hold onto them when they come to you. Don't turn them away. And definitely don't tell them they dress funny in front of the whole class.

T.J. I'm sorry, I'm really sorry. It just came out.

MR. FRANKLIN. We all see something so great in you, kid. We all believe in you. And the struggles you go through now are just going to make you that much greater. Do you hear me?

T.J. Yes.

MR. FRANKLIN. Good. Are you ready to go back to class?

T.J. Yeah.

MR. FRANKLIN. Come on.

(**MR. FRANKLIN** *walks off.* **T.J.** *follows for a while, but turns back to us and doesn't exit.*)

T.J. I'll never forget Mr. Franklin. He was the best teacher I ever had.
Later that day, I saw Sandy.

(**SANDY** *enters.*)

SANDY. I was crying all weekend. I'm so sorry I said it. I like you so much. I don't want you to hate me.

T.J. I don't hate you. I... like you.

SANDY. You like me? Like you *like* me like me?

T.J. Yeah.

I wrote a song about you.

SANDY. You did?

T.J. Yeah. And I want to tell you everything about me. I've never told anyone, but I want to tell you. If you still want to hear.

SANDY. Yes. You really wrote a song about me?

(His guitar magically appears and he sings.)

T.J.

EVERY NIGHT I DREAM
THAT YOU MIGHT LIKE ME
WHAT SHOULD I DO
I THINK I LIKE YOU

(She is in a daze.)

Well? What do you think?

SANDY. I wonder what you're gonna be when you grow up.

T.J. Grow up?

SANDY. You know. Like if you'll be a rock star or a poet or the President. Maybe all three.

T.J. Maybe. *(To us.)* And right then, I felt like maybe I could be. That I could really become anything I wanted.
Now it's two years later. The day of middle school graduation. Sandy's the valedictorian. She's just finishing her speech.

SANDY. *(Speaking as the valedictorian, with a graduation cap.)* And that's how you can learn the most: By just getting to know different kinds of people and accepting them for who they are. Thank you.

(General applause.)

T.J. I have a part to play in the graduation, also.

*(**MR. FRANKLIN** enters.)*

MR. FRANKLIN. And now, ladies and gentlemen on the verge of high school, it gives me great pleasure to introduce... the one and only... Thomas J. and the Declarations!

(**MOM** *enters, wearing sunglasses, gives another pair to* **SANDY**. *They become the* **DECLARATIONS**.)

T.J. Ready, girls?

SANDY. Ready.

MOM. Hit it kid.

T.J.

SOMETIMES YOU GET SO YOU CAN'T EVEN THINK
SOMETIMES YOU GET SO DISTRACTED
YOU OPEN YOUR EYES AND YOUR MIND'S DONE A BLINK
YOU GET USED TO IT AFTER THE PRACTICE

AND I'M HYPER
AND I'M FOCUSED
AND I'M... HYPER-FOCUSED
THEN I COME BACK DOWN
AND THERE'S LOVE ALL AROUND
AND I KNOW THAT THERE'S NOTHING THAT'S HOPELESS

SOMETIMES YOU TRY NOT TO SEE ANYONE
LIKE YOU LOOK IN THE SUN JUST TO FOCUS
THEN YOU LOOK ALL AROUND AND YOU SEE EVERYONE
AND YOU REALIZE IT ISN'T SO HOPELESS

AND I'M HYPER
AND I'M FOCUSED
AND I'M...HYPER-FOCUSED
THEN I COME BACK DOWN
AND THERE'S LOVE ALL AROUND
AND I KNOW THAT THERE'S NOTHING THAT'S HOPELESS

HYPER FOCUS!

(end of play)

Acting Edition

Hyper-Focus

by Jim Knable